Walt Disney®

TELL ME A STORY

S0-CIF-506

WALT DISNEY FUN-TO-LEARN LIBRARY

Cinderella

Long ago, in a far away kingdom, lived beautiful Cinderella with her stepmother and her two ugly stepsisters, Drizella and Anastasia. She did all the housework for her jealous stepsisters, who made her wear rags and sit in the cinders to keep warm.

In the kingdom, there lived a lonely prince. The king decided to invite all the unmarried girls to a ball so that the prince could choose a wife. The stepsisters were going, and Cinderella wanted to go with them.

This book belongs to

_____

But she didn't have a pretty dress to wear. When her stepmother realized that Cinderella wanted to go, she said, smiling wickedly, "First you must wash the windows, scrub all the floors, clean the drapes, and dust the chandeliers. If, when you have finished your work, you have time to make a suitable dress, of course you may go to the ball."

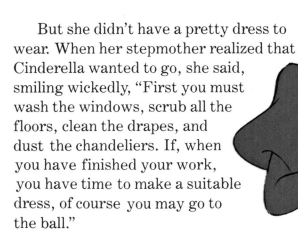

Cinderella knew she would never have enough time to make herself a ball gown. Sadly, she began to do all the chores. But her friends, the mice, had also heard the stepmother's words. Chattering excitedly, they collected ribbons and beads thrown into the garbage by Drizella and Anastasia, and made a beautiful ball gown for Cinderella out of an old dress they found in her cupboard.

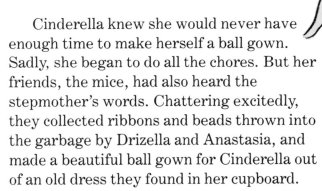

As Cinderella ran down the stairs in her new dress, her stepmother and stepsisters were furious to see how lovely she looked. "Those are my beads!" and "That's my ribbon!" they shrieked, as they tore Cinderella's dress to pieces.

As they drove away to the ball, Cinderella ran into the garden, sobbing. Suddenly, a glow of twinkling lights appeared, and Cinderella's Fairy Godmother popped out of thin air. "There's no time for crying," she said, as she waved her magic wand. "Bibbidi, bobbidi, boo!" — a garden pumpkin turned into a coach, Gus and Jaq and the other mice became horses, and Bruno the dog became a handsome footman. Cinderella's rags turned into a beautiful ball gown, and her old shoes became sparkling glass slippers.

"Be sure you leave by the stroke of midnight," warned Cinderella's Fairy Godmother. "For that is when the spell is broken."

When Cinderella arrived, the ball had already begun. The prince was bowing to the 210th and the 211th eligible young ladies, Drizella and Anastasia. Stifling a yawn, he suddenly looked up and saw Cinderella. He walked right past her two stepsisters and, taking her by the hand, began to dance with her. Cinderella and the prince danced every dance together while everyone else at the ball wondered who the beautiful girl might be. Seeing that his plan had worked, the king laughed happily — the prince had found the girl of his dreams.

Suddenly, Cinderella heard the clock begin to strike midnight. "I must go," she gasped. She turned, and ran down the palace steps. The prince ran after her calling, "STOP! I do not know your name." But Cinderella kept running. She lost one of her glass slippers, but it was too late to pick it up. The last bell rang out as Cinderella dashed through the palace gates.

When the guards ran after her, all they saw was a ragged girl sitting next to a smashed pumpkin, an old dog, and some mice.

The next day, the grand duke was sent all through the kingdom to look for the girl whose foot would fit into the glass slipper. When he came to Cinderella's house, her stepmother thought it best to lock Cinderella in her room. There was indeed something very suspicious about the way she had been singing and dancing all morning.

"Please, please let me out," cried Cinderella, rattling the door. But her stepmother, laughing wickedly, dropped the key into her pocket and walked away. She didn't know that Gus and Jaq were watching. Quietly, they followed the stepmother down the stairs.

As Drizella and Anastasia each tried to crush a large foot into the tiny slipper, Gus and Jaq stole the key from the stepmother's pocket. They let Cinderella out of her room just in time.

The grand duke was about to leave as Cinderella appeared on the stairs. "May I try on the slipper?" she asked. Seeing Cinderella, her stepmother tripped the duke, and the slipper smashed to the floor in a thousand pieces. Gus and Jaq gasped in horror, but Cinderella smiled. She pulled the other slipper out of her pocket and slipped it on her foot. It fit perfectly.

Just then, Cinderella's Fairy Godmother appeared. With a wave of her magic wand, and a "Bibbidi, bobbidi, boo," she transformed Cinderella's rags into the magnificent gown of the night before. Now, everyone could see that she was the beautiful girl with whom the prince had fallen in love. Cinderella's stepmother and stepsisters were furious, but there was nothing they could do to stop Cinderella from driving off to the palace.

There, with great rejoicing, she and the prince were married, and they lived happily ever after.

The Tortoise and the Hare

One day, a tortoise was going slowly down the road when a hare
zoomed along beside him. When the hare saw the tortoise, he stopped and
ran circles around him, laughing as hard as he could.

"Oh, brother, are you ever slow," whooped the hare. "I could get from
here to China and back before you'd moved six feet!"

"I'm not so slow," said the tortoise. For you see, he knew the hare, and he also knew that the hare could never stick to anything for more than a minute or two.

"Let's have a race," said the tortoise. "I'll race you to the lake."

"You've got to be kidding," said the hare, dancing around.

"Not at all," said the tortoise. "On your mark, get set, GO!"

Off dashed the hare, leaving the tortoise in a cloud of dust. But the hare had not gone too far when he felt a little tired.

"I'll take a nap for a few minutes," he said to himself. "That tortoise will take hours to get to the lake." And he fell asleep.

Meanwhile, the tortoise plodded along slowly but surely. Soon, he passed the hare sleeping by the side of the road. And the tortoise kept right on going.

As the sun began to sink lower in the sky, the hare woke up. He rubbed his eyes, and then he remembered the race. Off he ran as fast as he could go. But he had slept far too long. When he got to the lake, the tortoise was sitting there waiting for him.

"What took you so long?" asked the tortoise, chuckling.

The hare was out of breath, and couldn't answer.

So, as you can see, slow and steady is the way to win the race.

Goofy's Strange Day

One day, the wind and the sun were squabbling over which one of them was the strongest.

"I'm definitely the strongest," said the wind, puffing out his cheeks. "Let's have a contest and settle this matter once and for all."

Well, just then Goofy came strolling down the road. "See him?" said the sun. "Let's agree that whoever can get his coat off first is the strongest. All right?"

"No problem," said the wind, and he started to blow. The trees bent over, and big waves rose up in the lake. Poor Goofy began to get so cold that he hugged his coat closer around him, and buttoned it up to the neck. The stronger the wind blew, the tighter he held on to his coat.

At last, the wind became tired. As the storm clouds drifted away, the sun started shining. The sun's rays became hotter and hotter, until Goofy finally had to take off his coat and carry it.

"What crazy weather!" Goofy said to himself. "First, everything is fine. Then, I'm so cold I have to button up my coat. Two seconds later, it's so hot I have to carry it. What next?"

"Well?" asked the sun. "Who got the coat off, eh?"

The wind didn't answer, but he had always been a poor loser. So, as you can see, gentle ways can sometimes be stronger than rough ones.

Bambi's First Words

Bambi was born early one spring morning in a little forest glade. As he stood up on his wobbly legs, a magpie perched on a nearby branch and cried, "What a beautiful child." She flew off, repeating the news as she went.

"It isn't every day," said the owl, "that a prince of the forest is born. Congratulations!"

"His name is Bambi," said his mother, proudly.

Soon, Bambi went exploring with his mother down the forest paths. He heard the voices of thousands of woodland creatures buzzing all around him.

"Good morning, Prince Bambi," called someone from overhead. Bambi looked up to see who was calling him. But he didn't watch where he was going, and the next thing he knew, he had tripped over a rock, falling flat on his face.

"Get up, Bambi," said a rabbit that was nervously thumping his foot. "Try again." As Bambi struggled to his feet, the little rabbit said, "My name is Thumper." Just then a bird flew overhead. Bambi looked up curiously. "Those are birds," said Thumper. "Say 'bird,' Bambi."

"Bur," said Bambi. "Bur, bur." All Thumper's brothers and sisters hopped around with excitement and the baby opossums giggled at the fun. The little prince had said his first word! "Bur, bur," said Bambi again. Then he finally got it right. *"Bird!"*

Just then, a butterfly came into the clearing and fluttered close to Bambi's head. "Bird!" said Bambi happily. "No, no," said Thumper. "That's a butterfly!"

Bambi was so excited, he jumped toward a bush of bright flowers that looked like the butterfly. "Butterfly!" he announced, proudly.

"No, no, no," said Thumper. "Those are flowers!" Bambi bent his head to smell the flowers, just as a tiny black-and-white head poked itself out of the bush. "Flower!" exclaimed Bambi.

"No, no, no," giggled Thumper, rolling in the grass with laughter. "That's not a flower. That's a skunk!"

But the shy little skunk liked his new name. "The young prince can call me Flower if he wants to. I don't mind," said the skunk, smiling. "In fact, I like it."

"Flower," Bambi repeated. "Flower." The skunk's little black eyes gleamed with pleasure.

Suddenly, there was a flash of lightning and the rumble of thunder in the distance. "I think I'd better go home now," said Thumper. "It's going to rain."

Bambi had no idea what "rain" meant, but the loud noise had frightened him. Thumper had scampered off home, so Bambi ran to his mother. Together, they made their way to the thicket where they lay down to sleep.

Bambi was soon awakened by the sound of raindrops and the fresh wet smell of the earth. "So this is rain!" he thought. He snuggled up to his mother as the lightning flashed and the thunder boomed closer. As he watched the rain pour down through the leaves, he thought about all he had learned that day. Then he fell back to sleep, thinking of all he would learn tomorrow.

The Three Little Pigs on the Farm

Practical Pig had a nice little farm. His brothers, Fiddler and Fifer, were supposed to help him with the work. But the other little pigs spent all their time playing and never did much work at all. Practical was sure they would never learn anything about farming as long as he did the work for them. So, one day in the spring, he told them he had to take a long trip.

"While I'm away," Practical said, "I want you to plant wheat in the field. Now, remember, there is a great treasure in that field."

The next day, Practical Pig hauled a sack of seeds out to the field and then walked away from the farm. And as they waved good-bye, Fifer and Fiddler remembered what their brother had said about the treasure. They each imagined gold and silver and jewels buried somewhere in the field. So, they rushed to the barn, got out their hoes and shovels, and started digging up the field. They worked very hard in the hot sun, but they turned over every inch of that field and didn't find even one penny.

"There's no treasure here," said Fifer, finally.

"Maybe Practical was tricking us," said Fiddler.

"I bet it was just some old-time story that Mom once told him," said Fifer.
So the boys amused themselves tossing handfuls of seed at each other in the field. And then they went home to supper, forgetting all about the treasure. But the wheat they had planted during their game began to grow thick and fat.

It wasn't a good year for most other farmers, but the field that Fiddler and Fifer had planted grew the best of all. When they took their wheat to market, they came home with stacks of money.

Then they realized what Practical had meant. All that hard work in the field looking for the treasure had turned and tilled the soil. And that was why their wheat had grown so well.

As so they learned that hard work is really the best way to get rich.

Pluto and the Bone

One day, Pluto found a great big juicy bone. He decided he'd better take it to the woods where he could enjoy it without being bothered by other dogs. So, off he dashed with the bone in his mouth. But he had to cross a bridge to get to the woods.

When he was in the middle of the bridge, he happened to look down and see his reflection in the water. But he didn't know that it was his reflection. He thought it was another dog, with what looked like an even bigger bone in *his* mouth.

Pluto decided he would scare the other dog and get that even bigger bone, too. Then he would have two big juicy bones. But, as soon as he opened his mouth to bark, his bone fell with a great splash into the water, and Pluto never saw it again. Instead of two bones, he had no bone at all.

So Pluto learned to hold on to the good things he had. For, as he discovered, something better might not be there at all!

The Country Cousin

Abner lived in a nice, quiet cornfield in the country. There was always plenty to eat, and he could play happily in the corn stacks all day long.

Then his cousin Monte, who lived in a fine, big house, invited Abner to come visit the big city and taste the good life.

When Abner arrived, Monte led him straight into the banquet room. There, a huge table was set with all kinds of cheeses, breads, meats, cakes, brightly colored gelatins, and strange bottles and jars.

First, Abner tried a big piece of Swiss cheese. Next, he tasted some celery. Then he ate a handful of whipped cream and a big blob of jam. "This stuff is delicious!" he cried. Then he saw an large jar. He didn't know what was in it, but he tried a huge mouthful, anyway. It was *mustard!* "Quick! I need a drink," he gasped, and drank a whole glass of soda pop in one gulp. "Whew, that stuff was hot!" he exclaimed.

But then, because he'd eaten and drunk so quickly, he got the most horrible, noisy case of the hiccups.

Monte was getting very worried because Abner's hiccups were so loud. "Shhh..." he hissed. You'll wake up the cat." But Abner was feeling so pleased with himself that he sauntered up to the cat and gave it a swift kick on the bottom. The cat woke up snarling and turned on Abner.

Monte dashed into his mousehole, leaving Abner all alone in the banquet room. Luckily, Abner hopped right out an open window, and slid down a drainpipe into the street. "Safe at last," he gasped.

But just then, a trolley wheel whizzed right by him. He dashed out of the way and almost got run over by a honking car. Then he dodged the car and was practically trampled by hundreds of big, stampeding feet.

"Get me out of this place," he squeaked. Finally, he hitched a ride to the city line. And from there, he dashed back to his nice, safe cornfield. "The splendors of city life, indeed," he thought, as he munched on a delicious kernel of corn.

"It is better to live in peace," Abner decided, "than to risk the dangers of a fancy life."

Donald and the Pail of Milk

Donald was helping Grandma Duck on her farm. One day, as he was walking along to market carrying a pail of milk, he started thinking.

"If I sell this pail of milk, I can buy eggs," he thought. "And when the eggs hatch, I'll have chickens. And those chickens will lay more eggs. And then all those eggs will hatch, and I'll have lots and lots more chickens.

"And if I sell all those chickens, I'll have enough money to buy a nice little car," he thought, happily, as he walked along.

"And everyone will see me driving along in my car, and Daisy will wave and ask me for a ride," he thought, as he smiled to himself.

As he thought about driving off with Daisy beside him, he forgot to look where he was going.

The next thing he knew, he'd slipped in a great, big, muddy puddle. The pail of milk fell to the ground, and the milk spilled all over.

So, as you can see, it doesn't pay to count your chickens before they hatch.

Snow White and the Seven Dwarfs

Once upon a time, a beautiful queen gave birth to a daughter who had skin as white as snow, lips as red as roses, and hair as black as ebony. Her parents called her Snow White. Soon after she was born, the queen died.

A year later, the king took a second wife. She was also very beautiful, but very vain. Every morning, she would ask her Magic Mirror the same question: "Mirror, mirror on the wall, who is the fairest of them all?" And the mirror would answer, "You, O queen, are the fairest in the land."

With each passing day, Snow White became lovelier. Indeed, she became so beautiful, the queen was afraid that one day Snow White would be fairer than she. So her wicked stepmother dressed Snow White in rags and made her do all the dirtiest work around the palace. But it was no use. One day, when the queen asked her mirror who was the fairest in the land, the mirror answered: "Her lips blood red, her hair like night, her skin like snow, her name—Snow White."

The queen was furious. She commanded her huntsman to take Snow White into the forest and kill her. But the huntsman couldn't bring himself to kill the beautiful child. So he let Snow White go, warning her never to return to the palace.

Snow White ran and ran until she came to a
little thatched house in a clearing. Inside
the house, she found seven dusty little
chairs, seven dirty bowls, and seven
little shirts that needed washing.
With the help of some friendly woodland
creatures, Snow White set about
cleaning, washing, and tidying up. When she went
upstairs, she found seven little unmade beds,
each with a name carved on it: DOC, HAPPY,
SNEEZY, DOPEY, GRUMPY, BASHFUL, and SLEEPY.
She started to make the beds, but she was so tired that
she soon fell fast asleep.

When the Seven Dwarfs who lived in the house returned home, they found Snow White fast asleep across their beds.

"She's mighty purty," said Sneezy, shyly. And with that, Snow White awakened. She told them all about her evil stepmother, the queen. Then she asked the dwarfs if she could live with them.

The kind dwarfs were delighted. And so, every day when they went off to work in the mine, Snow White cooked and tidied up the little cottage. And every day, they warned her never to let a stranger enter while they were gone.

Meanwhile, the queen thought Snow White was dead. But one day, she asked her Magic Mirror her usual question, and the truthful mirror replied: "Over the seven jeweled hills, beyond the Seventh Fall, in the cottage of the Seven Dwarfs, dwells Snow White, the fairest of them all."

The queen was furious. She disguised herself as an old peddler. Then she went to a secret room in the castle and made a poisoned apple. Pleased with her clever plan, she set out for the cottage of the Seven Dwarfs.

Just at that very moment, the dwarfs were setting out for work. "Don't let anyone into the house," they warned. But no sooner were they out of sight, than the wicked queen knocked on the window and asked Snow White for a glass of water. Foolishly, Snow White came outside to give the old woman a drink. "Thank you, my pet," said the queen, as she handed back the glass. "Here is a beautiful red apple to reward you for your kindness."

Meanwhile, the dwarfs, warned by the friendly woodland animals, came racing back to the cottage. But it was too late! As soon as Snow White took a bite of the apple, she fell to the floor as if she were dead.

The dwarfs saw the wicked queen running into the woods, and ran after her as fast as they could. They chased her to the top of a high cliff, and there Snow White's cruel stepmother tripped and fell off the edge.

The dwarfs hurried back to Snow White, whose lips and cheeks were still rosy, as if she were asleep. She looked so lovely that the dwarfs placed her in a beautiful glass case. They laid it in a forest glade where they could keep watch over her day and night.

Time passed, and then one day a handsome prince heard about the beautiful princess and her glass coffin in the forest. Wanting to see for himself, he rode into the woods where Snow White lay. Overcome by her beauty, he immediately fell in love with her, and leaned over to kiss her lips. As he did so, Snow White's eyes fluttered open. The spell of the poisoned apple had been broken by love's first kiss. Snow White and the prince rode off together to his castle in the clouds while the dwarfs and the woodland creatures cheered.